TALES FROM
ONE STREET OVER

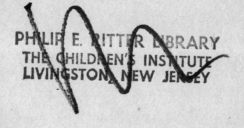

MELISSA WHITCRAFT lives in Montclair, New Jersey, with her husband, their two sons, and their dog. *Tales From One Street O er* is her first Avon Camelot book. She has also published *Francis Scott Key: A Gentleman of Maryland* for middle-grade readers.

TALES FROM
ONE STREET OVER

MELISSA WHITCRAFT

Illustrated by Jos. A. Smith

AN AVON CAMELOT BOOK

TALES FROM ONE STREET OVER is an original publication of Avon Books. This work has never before appeared in book form. This work is a novel. Any similarity to actual persons or events is purely coincidental.

AVON BOOKS
A division of
The Hearst Corporation
1350 Avenue of the Americas
New York, New York 10019

First Avon Young Camelot Printing: June 1994

CAMELOT TRADEMARK REG. U.S. PAT. OFF. AND IN OTHER COUNTRIES, MARCA REGISTRADA, HECHO EN U.S.A.

Printed in the U.S.A.

OPM   10 9 8 7 6 5 4 3 2 1

For Ben, Thomas, and Steven, with love

Contents

1
Michael Moves in

Michael peeked out from behind the living room curtains. Across the street four kids were riding bikes. "Boy," he whispered, "I wish I could do that!"

Just then the kids looked over at Michael's house as if they'd heard him. He dropped the curtain. He'd only been in the neighborhood a day. The last thing he wanted was for someone to think he was a sneak. What he did want was to join the fun, but he didn't know how.

1

He left the window and went upstairs.

His mom smiled when she saw him. "Look what they've done now," she said, pointing to a messy pile of sheets and towels at her feet.

Michael's three-year-old twin sister and brother giggled from behind her knees. His mom laughed and went back to folding laundry. How could they all be so happy when he felt so terrible?

He didn't care about the new house, his own bedroom, or a backyard big enough for playing catch. He wanted to be back in the city playing freeze tag in the park.

The kids outside laughed.

His mom looked up. "Want me to take you over to say hello?"

"No!" Michael shouted, stomping into his room. Didn't she realize they'd think he was a baby if she did that?

He picked up a book his parents had given him about moving. It was about a timid rabbit who made friends in a neighborhood of raccoons. But Michael wasn't a rabbit. The bike

2

riders weren't raccoons. They were kids, and Michael was scared.

"I hate this place," he cried, slamming the book down. "I want to go home!"

"This *is* home," said his mom, standing in the doorway with her arms crossed. "Now, play with the twins, unpack your toys, or go outside. Do anything. Even help me, but stop moping around feeling sorry for yourself."

Michael's eyes stung. He squeezed them shut and listened for city sounds. Honking horns, police sirens, or people walking on the sidewalk below. All he heard were the cheerful shouts of the bike riders.

Suddenly he had a great idea. If he had a reason to go outside, he could meet the kids without looking as if he wanted to. Then if they were unfriendly, he'd simply come back into the house and bug the twins.

"I'll take the garbage out," he said, grabbing a brown packing box. Willie, the family cat, leaped out of the box and ran under Michael's bed.

"Wait," Michael's mom called, "I want to save that box."

3

It was too late. Michael was already on the front lawn. Whistling, he dumped the box into the big garbage can his dad had dragged out to the curb earlier.

The kids across the street stopped playing and watched him.

Michael whistled louder. After all, not every seven year old can whistle.

The kids crossed the street with their bikes. Michael pretended to be very interested in a scratch on the side of the garbage can.

"Hi," said a voice behind him.

Michael took a deep breath and turned around.

"What's your name?" asked a girl with bright, red hair.

"Michael. What's yours?"

"Alison. That's Adam." Alison pointed to the boy with glasses standing next to her.

"I'm Jesse," the other boy said, raising his baseball cap in a wave.

"And I'm Sarah," said the other girl. She had short, curly hair. "I live next door to you. Are your sister and brother twins?"

4

Michael nodded.

"I thought so," Sarah said. "They're cute."

Michael smiled. "They're a zoo."

Sarah laughed.

"What grade are you going into?" Alison asked Michael.

"I hope first," said Adam. "No one around here is going into first except me."

Michael shook his head. "Second," he said.

"Same as me," said Sarah.

"You'll probably get Mr. Ferguson," Alison said. "I had him last year. He's mean."

"Oh," said Michael in a quiet voice.

"Don't listen to her," Jesse said. "Alison likes to scare people. I had him last year, too. He's okay."

"We're going over to the park," Adam said. "Why don't you get your bike and come with us?"

Michael hesitated. His bike was old, rusty, and pink. It had belonged to his cousin. His dad had said he could get a new one once they were settled. But the bigger problem was Michael hadn't learned how to ride a two wheeler yet.

"You do have a bike, don't you?" Alison asked.

"Sure," said Michael, blushing. "But it's not a two wheeler."

Alison laughed. "What is it, a tricycle?"

Michael's face got redder. "No. It's a . . . a unicycle."

Their mouths all dropped open.

"My dad's in the circus," Michael said quickly. "A trapeze artist." He scratched his cheek. His face always itched when he made up stories.

"Wow," said Adam. "A trapeze artist."

"And I ride a unicycle," Michael said. "Nobody cares about bicycles in the circus."

Alison scowled. "Show us."

"Show you what?"

"Your unicycle."

"It's not here," Michael stuttered. "It's with the rest of our circus stuff."

"I don't believe you," Alison said. "I'm going to ask your mom right now." She started for the house.

"No," Michael said. "Please don't. She's busy."

7

Alison crossed her arms. "Just as I thought. You're lying."

"I'm not," Michael said, fighting tears. "I'm not."

Adam shook his head.

Jesse and Sarah took a step towards him.

"Leave me alone," Michael cried, running into his backyard. "Just leave me alone."

He sat down on his back steps and cried. It was stupid to lie, but how could he admit that he'd never ridden a two wheeler? Who would want to play with him then?

He wiped his eyes and looked up. The kids were standing in his driveway.

"Go away," Michael yelled.

"Alison has something she wants to say," said Sarah, pushing Alison forward.

"I shouldn't have teased you," Alison said. "If you can ride a unicycle, that's great."

Michael peeled paint off the porch rail. "Well, I used to know how," he said. "When I was younger."

The others looked at each other.

"Okay." Michael peeled more paint off the

rail. "I can't ride a unicycle. I can't even ride a two wheeler. We're not in the circus. Dad works in an office. I said all those things so you'd like me. And if you don't want to be my friends now, that's fine." He stood up to go back into his house.

"Well, all I know," said Sarah quickly, "is that all this circus talk has made me hungry for popcorn. Anyone want to come over and make some?"

"Awright!" said Alison and Adam together.

Jesse turned to Michael. "Sarah's babysitter is the best cook. If we make the popcorn, I bet we can get her to bake cookies. Want to come?"

Michael smiled for the first time that day. "I'll be right there," he said.

He ran into his house. "Mom? Hey, Mom?"

She was in the bathroom vacuuming up the powder the twins had poured out.

"Can I go to Sarah's house?" Michael asked. "She's next door and everyone's going."

His mom wiped his bangs off his forehead. "Sure."

Michael started out.

She held him back. "Listen, I shouldn't have yelled. I know how hard this move has been for you."

"That's okay. Can I go now?"

She smiled. "Go."

Michael raced for the door. Then he stopped. "I was wondering, can the twins sleep in my room tonight? Just for old time's sake?"

"I don't see why not," said his mom.

"Awright!" Michael headed for the door again. He stopped again. "Oh yeah, one more thing. We'd better tell dad we're settled because I can't ride that old rusty bike. It's pink. And what about a unicycle? Think we can get one of those?"

His mom laughed and waved him off. "Michael, go."

Michael ran out the back door.

Jesse had waited for him. He was holding Michael's baseball bat. "You play?" he asked.

"Are you kidding?" said Michael. "I'm the home run king of my block."

Jesse frowned.

"I mean," said Michael, "I want to be a home run king."

Jesse laughed. "Yeah, me too. Come on, I'll show you the way."

"You know," said Michael, following him. "Maybe living here isn't going to be so yukky after all."

2
Rufus's Basket

Sarah loved snakes and snails and slugs. She also loved dogs, cats, birds, fish, horses, whales, and bugs. When she grew up, Sarah was going to be a veterinarian. In the meantime she planned to fill her house with pets. To practice.

The problem was her parents got a divorce last year. Sarah's mother worked full time now, and she didn't want any animals in the house. Not any.

"They're too much trouble," she said.

"Not hermit crabs," said Sarah.

"Hermit crabs are ugly," said her mother.

But Sarah saved her allowance and bought two hermit crabs anyway.

Her mom tapped lightly on the side of their clear, plastic box. The crabs retreated further into their shells. "Well, okay," she said.

Sarah's next addition, after her ant farm which she kept in the garage, was an aquarium. All the fish did quite well until the twins wandered over and fed them a box of sugar. Sarah returned from the first day of school to find the aquarium thick with seven stinking, sugar-coated swordtails.

She definitely needed a new pet. She wanted a snake, but her mom fainted at the thought. Cats were out because they clawed furniture and made Sarah's mom sneeze.

A dog seemed a better possibility. Sarah's mom liked dogs. When they took walks together, she stopped to pet the ones in the neighborhood.

Sarah went to work. She saved her allowance. She helped an elderly neighbor with his gardening. She even helped Michael's mom with the troublesome twins. Soon she had enough money to buy a wonderful, wicker dog basket.

She wanted to show it to her mom, but every night after supper, her mom spread pages of work over the kitchen table. She forgot Sarah was there.

One night when her mom remembered to come up and say goodnight, she noticed the wicker basket at the foot of Sarah's bed. "What's that for?" she asked.

"Rufus," said Sarah, sitting up.

"Rufus?"

"My dog."

"You don't have a dog, do you?"

"Not yet," said Sarah. "But—"

"Not ever," interrupted her mom. "A dog's the last thing we need around here."

"I'll pay for it."

"It's not only the expense," said her mom. "When you have a dog, someone has to be home to walk it. No one's here during the day."

"What about Miss Becker?" Sarah asked.

"She's only here in the afternoons."

"Daddy would let me," said Sarah.

"That's not fair," said her mom softly.

Sarah didn't care if she was being fair or not. It's not like she'd asked for a horse or an elephant. Only a little puppy. But the truth was, her dad wouldn't let her have a dog either. He couldn't. He lived in an apartment building that didn't allow pets.

Adam's collie, Comet, barked in the distance.

Sarah wanted to tell her mom that she missed her dad, but she couldn't find the right words.

Comet barked again.

Sarah's mom pulled down the shade and came to sit on her bed. "Look, I just can't manage a dog. Not now." She pulled Sarah's blanket up under her chin.

"When you say, not now," Sarah asked, "do you mean, maybe some day?"

Her mom smiled. "I guess I do." She leaned down and kissed Sarah on the forehead.

Sarah snuggled under her covers and fell

asleep wondering how soon her "some day" would come.

As it turned out, it came sooner than Sarah had expected. The next afternoon a beautiful, friendly golden retriever followed her home from school. He wasn't a puppy, exactly, but he wasn't full grown either.

"Goodness," said Miss Becker when she answered the door. "Who's this?"

"Rufus," said Sarah.

"You'd better leave him outside," Miss Becker said, pointing a wooden spoon at him. "Come on, I'm baking cookies."

"Great. Rufus loves cookies." Sarah yanked a reluctant Rufus into the kitchen.

A reluctant Miss Becker followed. "Your mother's going to hit the roof."

"She'll love him," said Sarah. She held out a spoonful of cookie dough to Rufus.

Whimpering, the dog lay down and put his head on his front paws.

"He's scared," said Miss Becker. She took hold of Rufus's collar and found his tag. "Here's his name. Finnigan."

"Finnigan?" said Sarah, "What kind of a name is Finnigan?"

At the sound of his name, Finnigan pricked up his ears.

Sarah laughed. "Okay, if Finnigan makes you happy, Finnigan it is."

Miss Becker picked up the telephone. "I'm going to call the number on his tag."

Sarah scratched the back of Finnigan's head. "Maybe his owner moved to some place where dogs aren't allowed."

"I'm still going to call," said Miss Becker.

Sarah led Finnigan upstairs. She didn't want to hear the conversation.

Finnigan sniffed around her room. To be safe, Sarah moved the hermit crabs out of his reach. When he found the basket, Finnigan circled it twice and curled up inside.

"You see," said Sarah. "A perfect fit."

Finnigan stood up and barked. He jumped onto Sarah's bed, knocked over a lamp, and grabbed her favorite stuffed animal between his teeth.

"Maybe you'd like to look at pictures,"

17

Sarah said, pulling the teddy bear out of his mouth.

She got down her photo album. It was filled with vacation shots. Sarah cartwheeling. Her mom hiking. Her dad leaping off rocks into the lake.

The doorbell rang.

Sarah closed the album. They wouldn't be going to the lake this summer.

When she looked up, Sarah saw Miss Becker standing in the doorway with a strange woman. Sarah knew who the woman was. So did Finnigan. He leaped and jumped all over her.

"Down boy, down," laughed the woman. "We were so worried." She turned to Sarah. "I can't thank you enough for finding him." She noticed the basket. "I see you have a dog, too."

Sarah's throat closed up.

"Well," said the woman. "I really have to get this guy home." She started down the stairs. Finnigan followed.

Sarah stayed on her bed. She heard the clip,

18

clip, clip, of Finnigan's nails on the stairs. She picked up her teddy. He was soggy, and one ear was torn. She looked at the soggy teddy, the basket, the overturned lamp, the photo album.

"Wait a minute," she called.

She ran downstairs. "Here, Finnigan should have this." Sarah handed the woman the wicker basket.

"What about your dog?" the woman asked.

"I don't have one," said Sarah. "Please, take it."

"Only if you promise to come visit Finnigan. Will you?"

"Sure." Sarah leaned down and gave Finnigan a hug. He licked her face and then scampered down the path after his owner.

Sarah's throat wasn't tight anymore.

She skipped back into the kitchen. On the table were two tall glasses of milk and two small plates. The cookies were done. Miss Becker was just taking them out of the oven.

Sarah picked up the phone to call her

dad. She wanted to ask him about Thanksgiving. He'd promised to take her to see the parade.

Then she'd call her mom and ask her if maybe, just maybe, she could have a hamster. She'd name him Finnigan.

3
The Thanksgiving Tooth

Adam was named after his father, his grandfather, his great-grandfather, and his great-great-grandfather.

His great-great-grandfather had made furniture. Once he had carried a couch on his back all the way across the Brooklyn Bridge.

His great-grandfather had owned a restaurant and sang songs for his customers.

His grandfather worked in a bank and had a telephone in his car.

His father was a teacher and sang in the church choir.

Adam was in the first grade and had a loose tooth. A very loose tooth.

He sat watching the Thanksgiving Day Parade on television. He wiggled his tooth with his tongue. In, out. Out, in.

Nicky, his little brother, sat next to him pretending he had a loose tooth, too.

"Four year olds don't lose their teeth," said Adam.

"Yes, I do," said Nicky.

"You're a pain," said Adam.

"No, I'm not," said Nicky.

"Granddad will be here any minute," said their mom. "And I want you to be especially nice this year. It will be hard for him without Grandma."

"But tell Nicky four year olds don't lose their teeth," said Adam.

"Oh, Adam," said his mom, picking up one of Nicky's toys, "What difference does it make?"

"A lot," said Adam. "It's my very first loose tooth."

His mom didn't answer. She was back in the kitchen.

"Wait till Granddad gets here," Adam said to Nicky. "He'll tell you."

Nicky didn't answer either. He was too busy watching the parade and wiggling his pretend loose tooth.

Adam went back to wiggling his tooth, too. With luck he'd have it out before Granddad got there.

The Thanksgiving Day Parade ended the same moment Granddad rang the doorbell. Adam raced to the door.

"Granddad," he yelled. "Guess what? Guess what?"

"Goodness," said Granddad, "what's all this about?" He patted Adam on the head and walked into the living room.

"Granddad, wait," said Adam, following him. "It's about my tooth. My very first loose tooth."

"Aha," said Granddad. "Here's my little tadpole." He lifted Nicky high above his shoulders.

Nicky giggled.

Adam was too heavy to be picked up any more. He pulled on his granddad's jacket. "Listen," he said.

But, Granddad couldn't listen. Everyone was talking at once. Adam's dad asked about the traffic. Nicky wanted to play, and Adam's mom had to explain that Adam was sleeping with Nicky to give Granddad a room of his own.

"I left you my superheroes," Adam interrupted. "In case you get lonely."

Granddad looked out the window. "I wish Grandma was here," he said softly.

Adam knew his granddad was sad because his grandma had died last summer. He thought his superheroes would cheer him up. But mentioning them had made his granddad feel worse.

Adam ran from the room. No one noticed.

When the other relatives arrived, Adam came downstairs and showed his loose tooth to all his cousins. But there were more important things to do than wiggle his tooth. There was turkey to eat and the wishbone to break.

After too much food, all the kids played

in the basement. Adam had so much fun he even enjoyed playing duck, duck, goose with Nicky.

Soon the day wound down. Night came. Cousins and aunts and uncles went home carrying leftover turkey and sweet potatoes, chocolate pilgrims, and candy corn.

The house was extra quiet after the wonderful noise of Thanksgiving. Adam's dad lit a fire in the fireplace. His mom put on her "chill-out" clothes.

Nicky sat on the rug scribbling on a pad of paper. Adam lay next to him reading a book.

Granddad read the newspaper. Every time he turned a page, he sighed.

Suddenly Nicky grabbed Adam's book.

"You brat," said Adam.

"Don't push," said his dad.

"Oh, great! He takes my book and I get yelled at!"

"Look, Adam," said his dad. "He shouldn't have taken your book, and you shouldn't have pushed him. Got it?"

Adam gave Nicky a dirty look.

Nicky started to cry.

"Enough!" Granddad shouted. He threw down his newspaper and stormed upstairs to Adam's room.

Everyone was quiet. Granddad had never acted that way before.

"He misses Grandma," said Adam's dad, putting his arm around Adam. "He's not mad at you."

"Come on," said his mom. "It's been a long day."

Upstairs, Adam stood outside the door to his room. He had to get his sleeping bag and pajamas out, but he was afraid to go in. What if his granddad yelled again?

He knocked very softly. There was no answer. He opened the door slowly and peeked in. Granddad was sitting on Adam's bed.

"Come, sit," he said.

Adam did.

Granddad showed him a photograph of Grandma. "I always sleep with this picture next to my bed," he said. "It was taken the

27

day of our wedding. Your great-grandfather had just finished singing a song."

Granddad put the photograph back on the bedside table. "This is the first Thanksgiving in forty-six years we haven't broken the wishbone together."

Adam started to cry.

"Hey," said Granddad, putting his arm around Adam. "What gives?"

"I miss Grandma, too," Adam cried. "If she were here, she'd listen to me."

"I'll listen," said Granddad.

"You haven't. Not all day." Adam took off his glasses and wiped his eyes. "You're only interested in the little tadpole."

"Oh," said Granddad, "I see." He moved closer to Adam. "I love you just as much as I love Nicky. My heart's big enough for both of you." He picked up one of Adam's superheroes. "Now, tell me what it is you wanted to say. I'll listen to every word. I promise."

Adam turned to face his granddad and grinned the biggest, toothiest grin he could.

Granddad smiled back and waited for Adam to speak.

Adam grinned harder.

So did Granddad.

Adam stuck his jaw way out and gave Granddad the biggest hint he could. He pointed right at the loose tooth.

"Oh, this is amazing." Granddad put on his glasses. "Yup. This tooth is going to come out any minute."

"You think?" Adam sat up straighter.

Granddad looked around the room. "What I need is some thread."

"I'll get some." Adam ran and got the sewing basket out of his parents' room.

Granddad found some black thread and tied a loop around Adam's loose tooth. He walked Adam to the door. "When your dad was a little boy," he said, "I tied one end of the thread around his loose tooth and the other end around a door knob. Then I slammed the door shut. When the door went, the thread followed, taking the tooth along for the ride. Shall we try it?"

Adam shook his head. He couldn't talk with the thread tied to his tooth, but this was definitely something he didn't want to do.

Granddad slammed the door anyway. *Bam!* The whole house shook.

Adam's dad ran up the stairs two at a time. "What happened?"

Granddad opened the door. Adam's entire family was standing on the other side.

Granddad smiled. "Everything's fine. Right, Adam?"

Adam felt for his tooth. It was gone. He looked at the door. One small, but very important tooth was dangling off the thread tied to the knob. He grinned at Granddad. "Yeah," he said. "Everything's fine."

Soon Adam was curled up in his sleeping bag in Nicky's room, his dog, Comet, at his feet. He kept sticking his tongue through the new hole between his teeth.

There were stories about all the other Adams in the family. Now there'd be one about him, too.

He reached under his pillow. No money yet.

"I hope I get enough to take Granddad for a milkshake," he whispered.

Nicky mumbled in his sleep.

"And maybe," Adam sighed, "maybe I'll buy a shake for the little tadpole, too."

4
'Tis the Seasons

It was the day after Christmas. Michael was miserable. He plopped down on the living room couch. There was no fire in the fireplace. The menorah stood empty on the mantle. The Christmas tree drooped under the weight of all its ornaments. The floor was littered with games and toys and books.

Michael had gotten some nice presents, but the one gift he really wanted hadn't been under either the menorah or the tree. Michael had not gotten a new bicycle.

He got up and walked to the window. Last night's blizzard had stopped. The whole street was silent under a thick blanket of snow.

"Michael?" His mother came up behind him. "Is everything okay?"

"I guess," said Michael, looking down.

"You're disappointed about the bike, aren't you?"

Michael nodded.

His mom put her arm around him. "I know it's difficult to understand, sweetheart, but as Dad and I explained, money's tight right now."

Michael bit his lip. It scared him when his mom said, "money's tight."

"But," she continued, leaning down to pick up some wrapping paper, "I'm sure things will get better soon."

There was a howl from the kitchen. Michael's mom ran off to rescue the cat from the twins.

Michael sat down. He promised himself he would stop thinking about bicycles. He took out his new, colored markers and drawing pad.

He began to draw. He whistled softly as the markers flew over the paper.

He looked down at his picture. It was hopeless. He had drawn a bright, red racing bike.

"Hey, sport, there you are." Michael's dad walked into the room, zipping up his coat. "Come on, if we hurry, we'll be the first ones down Hurricane Hill."

Michael jumped up. He loved sledding with his dad.

In the hall his mom was struggling with the twins. Each time she got a snowsuit on one, the other's came off.

As Michael snapped up the front of his jacket, the telephone rang. His dad answered it.

He came back unzipping his jacket. "So much for having the day off. They want me to run through the charts again."

"When are they going to make up their minds?" Michael's mom asked.

Michael's dad kissed her on the cheek. "At least they haven't said no yet." He went back upstairs to his desk.

Michael started to undo his jacket.

"Oh, no you don't." His mom stopped him. "You're going out for some fresh air."

Before Michael knew what had happened, he was standing on the front steps. The cold took his breath away.

Jesse waved from his front yard.

Michael waved back and ran across the street. His footprints left the first marks on the snow.

"Let's make a fort," said Jesse, packing snow into a wall.

"Yeah," said Michael. "Ten feet high."

The cold seeped through Michael's gloves and made his fingers ache. But, the work drove his red racing bike out of his mind.

Jesse stepped back. "What do you think?" he asked, jumping up and down to keep warm.

"It's not exactly ten feet yet," said Michael, stepping over the wall.

"It's close enough," said Jesse. He ran towards his house. "Come on. Let's get some cocoa."

A few minutes later the two were warming

their hands around steaming cups of hot chocolate.

Michael noticed that Jesse had a candleholder that looked like a menorah. "Hey," he asked, "are you guys Jewish?"

"Jewish? Michael, we're African-American."

"But you have a menorah."

"That's a kinara for Kwanzaa."

"Kwanzaa?"

"It's a special holiday when African-Americans celebrate their heritage," Jesse said. "We light a candle every day for seven days and talk about the special principle that day represents."

Jesse bit into a marshmallow. "We also talk about famous African-Americans and eat great food. And on the last day, we get presents. Usually neat stuff about our heritage, but sometimes other things, too."

He leaned over so his mom wouldn't hear. "The best part about celebrating both Kwanzaa and Christmas is that if you don't get a present for one, you can get it for the other."

"That usually happens with us, too," said Michael. "Since Mom's Jewish and Dad's Christian. But not this year."

Michael took a sip of cocoa and told Jesse what he hadn't gotten for the holidays.

"Maybe you can get a unicycle for Kwanzaa," Jesse laughed.

Michael blushed. He didn't like to be reminded of his first day in the neighborhood.

Just then the telephone rang. Michael's mom wanted him to take the twins out into the backyard.

Back at his house Michael heard his parents arguing upstairs. They had been arguing all week. It made Michael's stomach hurt.

The twins, sweating in their snowsuits, were sitting quietly on the stairs. They hated it when their parents fought, too.

Michael took one twin in each hand. "Come on," he said, "we'll build a snowman."

The snow packed beautifully, but within three minutes the twins were frozen. Within four minutes all three were back inside watching TV.

Halfway through the twins' favorite show, their dad wandered in. "Aha," he said, sitting next to Michael. "Just the break I need." He patted Michael on the knee and tickled the twins. He watched the cartoons and laughed.

Michael thought he laughed too long and too loud to be really happy.

In the distance the telephone rang. Michael's mom came into the room. "Jesse and his family have invited us for over Kwanzaa," she said.

Michael's dad sighed. "I'm beat."

"It will do us good," said Michael's mom. She patted Michael's dad lightly on the shoulder. "I'm going to make dessert. Michael, want to help?"

Michael thought of mentioning that kids get presents at Kwanzaa, just to remind his parents about his bike. But, he knew they weren't thinking about presents at the moment. He got up to help his mom.

That night when it was time to go to Jesse's, Michael's mom and the twins went over first, carrying a chocolate layer cake. Colored

Christmas lights shone softly through snow heavy bushes.

Michael's dad locked the front door and took in a deep breath. "Well," he said. "This certainly wasn't the holiday season I expected."

"Me neither," said Michael.

His dad put his arm around Michael's shoulder. "Sorry about the bike."

"That's okay." Suddenly Michael didn't care about his bike anymore. He was afraid his dad was going to lose his job.

"Is everything okay at work?" he asked.

"Well, it doesn't look like they're going to use my idea," his dad said. "But they did appreciate the hard work I put into it."

"Is that good?" Michael asked.

His dad nodded. "That's good." He made a snowball and threw it across the street. "In fact, that's so good that when all this white stuff melts, you and I will go hunting for the best bike around."

"That's great, Dad, thanks." Michael hugged him. "Hey, Happy Kwanzaa."

"Thanks, sport, same to you. Happy Kwanzaa, Merry Christmas, Happy Chanukah, and Happy, *Happy* New Year!" He laughed.

It was a deep, warm, real laugh, and Michael knew his mom had been right. Things would get better. He grabbed his dad's hand. Together they raced across the street.

Jesse opened the door. A shaft of golden light shot out across the snow. Michael and his dad walked into the house and joined the laughter inside.

Jesse shut the door. The street was dark and quiet once more.

5
The
Second Greatest Pitcher
in the Major Leagues

Jesse lived for baseball. He knew all the stats of all the players on all the teams. What he didn't know he looked up. He and his brother, Paul, had a whole bookcase full of baseball biographies, baseball encyclopedias, baseball histories, and baseball novels.

At night, instead of asking Paul to tell him ghost stories, Jesse asked for tales of baseball. Tales Paul knew only too well because he was as big a baseball nut as his little brother.

Paul was a pitcher for the high school freshman team. Jesse liked nothing more than catching for him when he practiced. Paul's wind-up was beautiful, his delivery outstanding.

Jesse believed Paul was going to be the greatest pitcher in baseball. When Paul gave him a pitcher's mitt for Kwanzaa, Jesse decided he'd be a pitcher too.

All winter he worked on his glove, shaping it fit his hand. He tied a baseball into it and rubbed the leather with linseed oil.

By April the mitt was ready. It was as soft and flexible as any pro's.

The first day of tryouts for the town league, Jesse hooked the mitt over his handle bars and rode off to the park. Apple blossoms fluttered down in front of him.

Jesse imagined he was at the center of a huge ticker tape parade. He smiled and waved. After all, he was an awesome pitching star. The greatest since his brother Paul.

When he got to the baseball diamond, Jesse walked out to the pitcher's mound. He swept the rubber clean with his cleats.

In Jesse's mind it was October. The stadium was roaring. One more strike and the game was his. Raising his arms over his head, the way he had practiced all winter, Jesse lifted his leg and let go with a perfect, if invisible, fast ball.

A piercing whistle brought him back from his series winning strikeout. Coach Turner waved all the players into the dugout. He smiled as Jessie jogged up.

"Guess there's another pitcher in the family," he said.

"Guess." Jesse shrugged, hiding a smile.

Besides Jesse there were two other guys trying out for pitcher. Everyone was rusty. Most of the balls went everywhere except over the plate. When one of Jesse's pitches hit a batter in the leg, Coach Turner took him out.

"Don't worry about it," he said, sending Jesse to right field. "It will come."

Jesse stood in right field and hit his fist into his glove. He'd ask Paul why his pitches weren't hitting the mark. Paul would know what to do.

After practice Jesse raced home to find his brother. He wasn't there. He'd gone out for pizza with some friends.

"He's never home anymore," Jesse said, storming out the kitchen door.

"No sliding practice," his mom called after him. "Dad's just seeded the lawn."

Jesse sat in the tire swing that hung from a tree in the bank yard. When he was younger, he had swung on the tire for hours. Now Paul used it for pitching practice.

Jesse slid out of the swing. "If Paul can do it, so can I."

He grabbed two buckets of old tennis balls from the garage, paced off pitching distance from the tire and started throwing pitches. He threw, and he threw, and he threw.

Two buckets later there were balls in the garden, balls in the garage gutter, and balls in the neighbor's wheelbarrow. Not one ball had gone through the tire.

Jesse wasn't hungry at supper. He went upstairs as soon as he could and waited for Paul. When Paul came in, he went straight to his desk.

"Paul, can I ask you something?" Jesse said. "I've been having a bit of trouble with my wind-up."

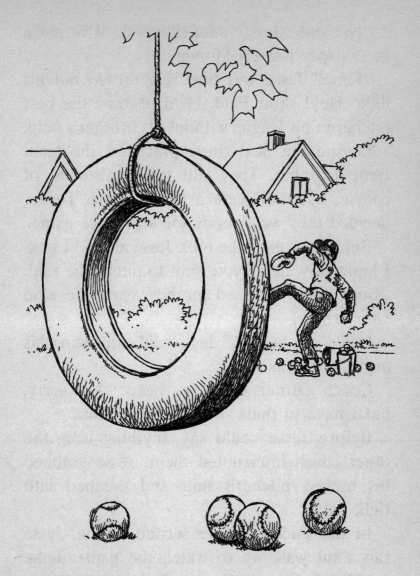

"Not now, Jess," Paul snapped. "I've got a huge paper due on Monday."

"Fine." Jesse was hurt. He turned out his light. He'd show Paul. He'd become the best pitcher in his league without his brother's help.

During the next three practices, the team came together. They still made mistakes, of course, but they were a team. Coach Turner decided they were ready for a practice game.

Before the game he took Jesse aside. "Look, I know how much you want to pitch," he said. "But I think you need another year to develop your arm."

"I'll work harder," Jesse said, squeezing his arms across his chest.

Coach Turner shook his head. "I'm sorry, but I have to think of the whole team."

Before Jesse could say anything else, the other coach interrupted them. Jesse grabbed his useless pitcher's mitt and escaped into right field.

In the middle of the second inning, Jesse saw Paul walk up to watch the game. Jesse couldn't believe it. For weeks he couldn't get his brother to help, and now here he was, just in time to see him exiled to the outfield.

Paul and the coach started laughing.

That did it. Jesse threw down his mitt and ran off.

He hadn't gotten very far when Paul caught up to him. "Hey, where are you going?" he asked.

"None of your business." Jesse walked faster.

Paul held out his mitt. "You dropped this."

Jesse knocked the mitt out of Paul's hand.

Paul picked it up. "You're a real jerk," he said.

"Who asked you?" Jesse answered, marching off again.

"No one leaves the field in the middle of an inning," Paul yelled after him.

Jesse stopped. "Maybe I don't want to play baseball," he yelled back. "Maybe I think baseball's a stupid game for stupid people like you. Maybe I hate baseball."

"You love baseball," Paul said softly.

Jesse kicked at the dirt. He didn't want Paul to see him cry. "He won't let me pitch."

"I know."

"And you laughed."

"Jesse, we were laughing about how no one wants to catch. Once a pitcher starts really flinging balls, no one ever wants to be on the other side of the plate."

Paul paused. "No one except someone who's practiced. Someone who knows more about pitching than most pitchers."

Jesse remembered all the hours he'd caught pitches for Paul. "Me?"

"Why not?" Paul asked. He turned back towards the dugout. "What do you say?"

Jesse's team was at bat. He was missing a chance to hit.

"A pitcher can't be a pitcher," Paul said, "without a great catcher. He can't."

"Yeah," Jesse said, taking his mitt from Paul. "He can't."

That afternoon Jesse played catcher the last inning of the game. It felt good. Really good.

When he got home later there was a note on the kitchen table. "Meet me at Pizza Heaven." The note was from Paul.

Jesse jumped on his bike and took off.

Alison came storming out of her house. "Yo, Alison," Jesse called as he went by.

Alison scowled.

Jesse shrugged and peddled faster.

At the restaurant Paul was sitting with his buddies. There was no room for Jesse.

Paul got up and moved to another table. "I ordered us a pizza," he said, sitting down.

"With anchovies?" Jesse asked, joining him.

Paul shuddered. "Yeah, with anchovies." He reached under the table and brought out a shopping bag. He handed it to Jesse. "It's not Kwanzaa, but hey, Happy April."

Jesse put his hand into the bag. He pulled out a fat, stiff, beautiful catcher's mitt.

Paul smiled and raised his soda. "To the greatest catcher–pitcher duo in the history of the game."

Jesse smiled and raised his soda, too. "Thanks," he said, as the waiter set down a hot, bubbling pizza loaded with anchovies.

6
Alison Moves Out

Alison woke up, but she didn't open her eyes.

"Breakfast," her mom called from the kitchen.

Alison's two older brothers ran down the stairs. Her dad slammed in from the back yard.

Alison didn't budge. She did open her eyes. Nothing had changed. Her walls were still bare, her bookcase still empty. It was the first week of summer vacation, and Alison was moving.

The whole mess started when Alison's mom started taking business trips to a far away city. When she came back, she and Alison's dad whispered in corners, stopping the minute Alison walked into the room.

One week both her parents went away. Miss Becker, Sarah's sitter, came to stay. She let Alison and her brothers watch TV on school nights, but Alison hated that week. The house felt empty without her parents.

When they returned, they had great news. Both had gotten new jobs in the city where Alison's mom grew up.

"It's a dream come true," her mom said.

To Alison it was a living nightmare, and if her parents thought she was going to move thousands of miles away, they'd better think again. Alison had dreams of her own.

She hopped out of bed and got dressed. Grabbing her backpack, she tiptoed downstairs and quietly slipped out the front door.

The street was empty. Early morning newspapers still lay unclaimed on everyone's front walk.

Inside Alison's brothers laughed at one of their jerky jokes.

She raced across the lawn and disappeared into Michael's back yard just as Adam came out to walk his dog. Quickly she ran behind Michael's garage.

There, built between the back wall of the garage and a snarled, old apple tree, was a small shack.

Alison crawled inside. It was dark and the ground was damp, but no one would look for her here.

She opened her backpack and pulled out a towel. She spread it out and sat on it. Then she pulled out two cans of soda, a bag of cookies, three slices of ham, a book, and a soft, well-hugged calico horse.

She sat her horse next to her, opened a soda, took one cookie, and leaned against the wall.

The neighborhood was waking up. Doors slammed and cars started. Parents were off to work.

Then everything was quiet again, until the

kids came out. Alison heard them calling from yard to yard. She sat further back in her corner.

Suddenly Michael was standing in the doorway of the shack. He ducked down and came in.

"Yikes," he shouted when he saw Alison.

"Shh," she whispered. "Not so loud."

"What are you doing in our clubhouse?" Michael asked. "The guys will kill me if they knew I let a girl in here."

Outside people were calling Alison's name. It drifted across the neighborhood like an echo. One voice got louder and louder. It was one of Alison's brothers. He was in Michael's yard.

Alison put her finger to her lips, begging Michael to keep her secret.

Michael stuck his head out the door.

Alison crossed her fingers.

"Hey, Mike," said Alison's brother. "Seen my sister?"

"Not really."

"Not really?"

"Ah," Michael stuttered, "I mean no. I

55

haven't seen her." He started to scratch his cheek.

"What's the matter with your face?"

"Nothing." Michael dropped his hand.

"Are you sure you haven't seen her?" Alison's brother stepped closer to the door.

Michael stepped in front of him. "I told you," he said. "I haven't seen her."

"Well, if you do, tell her Mom and Dad want her home now! The moving van's here. We can't spend the rest of the day looking for her." He walked off into Sarah's yard.

Alison uncrossed her fingers and started to cry.

"What's going on?" Michael asked.

"I'm not moving," Alison said, wiping her eyes.

"You have to," Michael said. "You can't stay here without your parents."

"Oh, yeah? I have it all figured out. I'll stay in here until Sarah gets back from visiting her dad. Then I'll move into her attic. I won't go to some stupid city, a trillion miles away."

"Cities aren't so terrible," Michael said. "I

lived in one before we moved here. They can be a lot of fun."

"Ha!" said Alison. Her eyes filled with tears. "I can't go. I can't live in an apartment. What am I supposed to do with my bike? And I won't have any friends. Not one."

"Hey," Michael said, jumping up. "I just thought of something." Before Alison could stop him, he ran out of the clubhouse.

Alison bit into another cookie. The shack smelled and there were huge cracks in the roof. Today, the sun filtered through in bright streaks. But, what would happen if it rained? She'd have to ask Michael for an umbrella.

She heard someone outside. "Michael," she whispered.

"No," said a familiar voice. "It's me." Alison's mom bent down and crawled into the shack.

Alison drew up her legs. "How did you find me?"

"Your brother got suspicious because Michael blushed when he asked him where you were."

"I'm not going," Alison said, getting right to the point.

"I gather." Her mom sat next to her. "I'm sorry you're so unhappy."

"You never even asked me if I wanted to go," Alison said.

Her mom was silent for a moment. "You're right. And that was wrong of me. Everything was moving so fast, Allie. We didn't have time to think. But, this move will be be so much better for us. All of us."

"For you."

"No, for our whole family. Daddy and I will have more time for you and your brothers. Uncle Chris and Aunt Molly live nearby. You'll have cousins to play with."

"But no friends," said Alison.

"You'll make new ones."

"I don't want new ones," Alison said. "I like my old ones."

Her mom hugged her. "I know it hurts."

Alison nodded. It did hurt. It hurt a lot. But talking with her mom helped. "What about my bike?" she asked, her eyes filling with tears again.

"What about it? The city has fabulous parks and bike trails. We can ride for miles and miles."

Alison smiled a little.

"And I promise," her mom said, "I will never keep anything from you again."

Alison picked up her calico horse. She was still angry, but maybe going would be better than staying here alone. At least the apartment wouldn't have a leaky roof. She put her calico horse into her backpack.

Her mom helped her stuff everything else back in and then they crawled out of the shack.

Michael was there. He handed Alison a book. "Maybe this will help," he said. "It's this goofy story about a rabbit who moves into a neighborhood of raccoons."

"Thanks, Michael." Alison took the book. "I'll miss you," she said quietly.

Michael blushed.

Alison looked over at Jesse and Adam. She laughed. "You guys look like it's the end of summer vacation instead of the beginning.

Smile. Moving's not the end of the world. I'll be back, and you can come visit me."

She started down Michael's driveway. In front of her house the moving men were just putting her bike into the van.

She looked back at her friends.

They waved.

She waved back and disappeared around the corner.

7
The Block Party

Michael looked out his living room window. Up and down the street neighbors had decorated trees with ribbons and balloons. Now they were setting up tables for the street's annual Fourth of July Barbecue. His mom and dad were lighting their charcoal grill.

Michael grabbed a shopping bag and ran out to his back yard.

Jesse was waiting with the other kids by the clubhouse. "It's about time," he said.

"I had to wait until Dad finished decorating the lamppost," Michael answered, dumping out the bag. Rolls of red, white, and blue streamers poured out onto the grass.

"This is juth thuper," said Adam.

Michael smiled. It was almost impossible to understand Adam these days. He had lost two more teeth since Thanksgiving. Both had come out using his granddad's door slamming technique.

Michael turned to Sarah. "Do you have the banner?" he asked.

"Yup." Sarah unrolled an old sheet. In big bold letters she had written HAPPY FOURTH OF JULY!

"Perfect," said Michael. "Now, pick your colors and get to it."

Everyone grabbed for the rolls. Sarah ran back to her house for something.

Adam finished his bike first. Then he turned to help Nicky with his scooter. "Granddad's going to love thith," he said as he hung streamers from the handlebars.

Michael's job took the longest. The twins kept pulling the streamers off their tricycles to decorate each other.

"If you guys don't knock it off," Michael said, "I will never, ever, let you watch 'Sesame Street' again."

The twins were instantly quiet and well-behaved.

Finally finishing their trikes, Michael turned to his bike, his new, beautiful, fire engine red bicycle complete with hand brakes and white, white tires.

Adam came up behind him.

"What do you think?" Michael asked.

"It'th beautiful," Adam said. "It'th the most beautiful bithycle I've ever theen."

"I know," said Michael, his eyes sparkling. "The second Dad and I saw it, we knew this was the bike for me."

When the bikes and trikes and scooter were done, each had been turned into a bright explosion of color.

"Excellent," said Jesse.

"Where's Sarah?" Michael asked, looking

around. "Our parents have started cooking. We gotta get going."

Just then Sarah came through the bushes carrying a small puppy. "I wanted him to wear a bow," she said, "but he has a mind of his own." She put the bowless puppy into the basket of her bike.

The dog jumped up and licked her face.

Sarah laughed. "Down, Rufus, down."

Michael clapped his hands. "Come on," he whispered, "let's go."

Jesse slipped his catcher's mitt over his handlebars and picked up one side of the banner.

Michael pulled up next to him and picked up the other side.

Nicky was next in line. He left his scooter behind. He had decided to be a band. In one hand he held a garbage can lid. In the other a stick. In his mouth was a large, wooden whistle.

Behind Nicky came the twins. With luck they'd stay together and not take off, as they usually did, in separate directions.

Sarah and Adam brought up the rear with their dogs, more or less dressed for the occasion.

Nicky started banging his lid and blowing his whistle. The parade began. Slowly, they all came down Michael's driveway to the street.

Michael's heart raced. Everything had to go right. It just had to.

He rode carefully, balancing the banner with one hand and steering with the other. He couldn't wait to see the expression on his parents' faces.

They had gotten him the bike in May and had given him a couple of lessons. To surprise them, Michael had spent the last few weeks really practicing with Jesse.

With only a slight wobble, Michael rode past his parents' table. They were more than surprised when they saw what he could do. They were astonished and proud. They broke into loud applause.

Michael flashed them a huge grin and turned the corner to lead the parade up the street.

All the parents ran off to get cameras and

video cameras. Babies too young to walk clapped at the curb. High school kids, who usually thought Michael and his friends were dorks, joined in the march.

The parade ended at the last house on the corner. There, the elderly gentleman Sarah helped garden had set up bouquets of flowers for the adults and helium balloons for the kids.

"Too bad Alison's not here," Jesse said. He tied his balloon to his bike.

"Didn't I tell you?" Sarah said, trying to keep her balloon away from her puppy, "I got a letter from Alison. She said the apartment is neat. It's so high it's like living in a bird's nest. Except that her nest has cable TV and an elevator."

Michael laughed. "That sounds like Alison."

Michael's dad waved from down the street. The hot dogs were ready.

Michael and his friends raced back to his house.

"Great parade," said his dad, handing him the mustard.

"Thanks," said Michael with a smile.

Later, Michael was taking his first lick of a homemade strawberry ice cream cone when he saw a car pull up in front of Alison's old house. A car with an overloaded trailer.

"Hey, guys, look," he said.

A man and a woman started unloading the trailer.

Some of the parents went up the street to help. They took down two adult bikes, one girl's bike, one boy's, a tricycle, and a stroller.

"Wow," said Adam, "They've got a lot of kidth."

The new girl looked over at Michael and his friends and hurried into the house.

"I wonder if she's nice," said Sarah, scratching Rufus behind the ears.

Michael saw the living room curtain move. He remembered his first day all those months ago when he had been too scared to come out. "Let's go," he said.

He walked over to the house. The others

followed. He rang the bell. The girl came to the door. Her baby brother was crawling around her feet. Two younger boys were playing on the stairs.

"Hi," said Michael. He handed the girl his balloon. "Welcome to our street."

FOR GREAT ON-THE-FIELD BASEBALL ACTION CHECK OUT ALL OF THESE ADVENTURES WITH

The Hit and Run GANG

(#1) NEW KID IN TOWN	76407-5/ $3.50 US/ $4.50 Can
(#2) PLAYING FAVORITES	76409-1/ $3.50 US/ $4.50 Can
(#3) THE SLUMP	76408-3/ $3.50 US/ $4.50 Can
(#4) THE STREAK	76410-5/ $3.50 US/ $4.50 Can
(#5) PITCHING TROUBLE	77366-X/ $3.50 US/ $4.50 Can
(#6) YOU'RE OUT!	77367-8/ $3.50 US/ $4.50 Can

Coming Soon

(#7) SECOND CHANCE	77368-6/ $3.50 US/ $4.50 Can

Celebrating 40 Years of Cleary Kids!

CAMELOT presents
BEVERLY CLEARY FAVORITES!

- ☐ **HENRY HUGGINS**
  70912-0 ($3.99 US/$4.99 Can)
- ☐ **HENRY AND BEEZUS**
  70914-7 ($3.99 US/$4.99 Can)
- ☐ **HENRY AND THE CLUBHOUSE**
  70915-5 ($3.99 US/$4.99 Can)
- ☐ **ELLEN TEBBITS**
  70913-9 ($3.99 US/$4.99 Can)
- ☐ **HENRY AND RIBSY**
  70917-1 ($3.99 US/$4.99 Can)
- ☐ **BEEZUS AND RAMONA**
  70918-X ($3.99 US/$4.99 Can)
- ☐ **RAMONA AND HER FATHER**
  70916-3 ($3.99 US/$4.99 Can)
- ☐ **MITCH AND AMY**
  70925-2 ($3.99 US/$4.99 Can)
- ☐ **RUNAWAY RALPH**
  70953-8 ($3.99 US/$4.99 Can)
- ☐ **RAMONA QUIMBY, AGE 8**
  70956-2 ($3.99 US/$4.99 Can)
- ☐ **RIBSY**
  70955-4 ($3.99 US/$4.99 Can)

- ☐ **STRIDER**
  71236-9 ($3.99 US/$4.99 Can)
- ☐ **HENRY AND THE PAPER ROUTE**
  70921-X ($3.99 US/$4.99 Can)
- ☐ **RAMONA AND HER MOTHER**
  70952-X ($3.99 US/$4.99 Can)
- ☐ **OTIS SPOFFORD**
  70919-8 ($3.99 US/$4.99 Can)
- ☐ **THE MOUSE AND THE MOTORCYCLE**
  70924-4 ($3.99 US/$4.99 Can)
- ☐ **SOCKS**
  70926-0 ($3.99 US/$4.99 Can)
- ☐ **EMILY'S RUNAWAY IMAGINATION**
  70923-6 ($3.99 US/$4.99 Can)
- ☐ **MUGGIE MAGGIE**
  71087-0 ($3.99 US/$4.99 Can)
- ☐ **RAMONA THE PEST**
  70954-6 ($3.99 US/$4.99 Can)
- ☐ **RALPH S. MOUSE**
  70957-0 ($3.99 US/$4.99 Can)